W9-CNA-115

How the chipmunk got its stripes

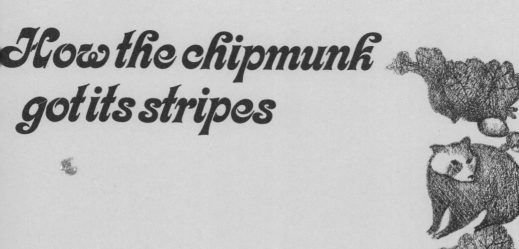

by Nancy Cleaver

illustrated by
Laszlo Gal

Clarke, Irwin & Company Limited/Toronto/Vancouver/1973

©1973 by Clarke, Irwin & Company Limited

ISBN 0-7720-0586-9

2 3 4 5 / 77 76 75

To the ancient story-tellers who watched the friendly chipmunks
and gave this legend to their tribes

Long ago when the world was young, a small red squirrel made friends with a boy.

In those days people were learning to use bows and arrows, and the animals feared and hated them. This made Manitou, the great spirit of the north woods, very sad. And when he saw the squirrel and the boy together he was pleased.

It all began late one winter—a colder, windier, icier winter than many years had seen.

The squirrel had eaten all the nuts and seeds she had stored in the hollow of the big beech tree where she lived. No matter where or how hard she looked, there was no food to be had. She was very hungry.

The boy saw the hungry squirrel and threw her an acorn. At first the squirrel was afraid and ran away, but when the boy didn't chase her, she grew bold. The boy threw her another acorn, then another. She grew bolder and bolder.

They became friends. They went for walks. They ate acorns and corn kernels. All through the sweet green spring they played together.

Then, one warm day in summer, the boy did not come out to play. After a long wait, the squirrel crept to the edge of the wigwam to see what was wrong. The boy was lying on his blanket. Squirrel chattered and scolded at him to get up, but the boy said, "It's no use, Squirrel. I can't play today."

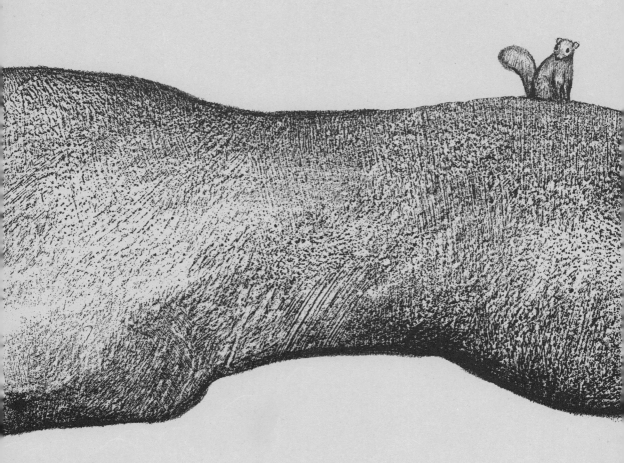

The squirrel didn't understand the words but she understood that something was wrong, and she was worried. She ran. As fast as she could run, she ran and brought the boy a ripe, red raspberry. The boy stretched out his hand for her gift, but his arm dropped down. He was very sick. His mother and father were sick too. For three days Squirrel brought berries to the family, but they did not get better.

Squirrel was afraid for her friend. She went in and out of all the wigwams in the village, but there was no one to help. Sickness was spreading through the tribe.

"Well," Squirrel said to herself, "there's only one thing to do. I'll have to ask the other animals."

She thought about them all, especially the bear, the big angry bear. Then she took a deep breath. She prayed a quick prayer to Manitou, and went to see the porcupine.

Porcupine was lying on a low limb of a willow tree at the edge of his favourite pond. He was reaching for the root of a water lily that floated under his branch.

"Porcupine," said the squirrel, "I have something to ask you."

The porcupine did not answer. He wanted the water lily root for his lunch, and he did not want to be interrupted while he fished for it.

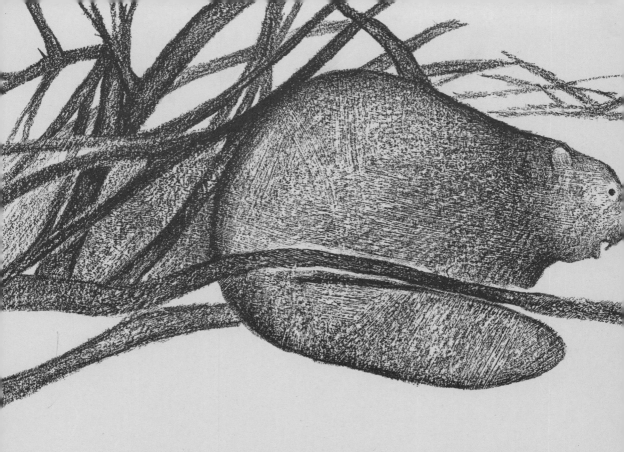

"Porcupine. It's me, your friend Squirrel. Will you call a council of the animals?" This time Squirrel spoke very loudly.

For a long time Porcupine said nothing, but his paw stopped reaching. Squirrel waited, trying not to show how impatient she was. Finally the porcupine asked, "Why?"

"I have a reason, Porcupine. It's important, but you know how little I am. They won't come for me. It's the first time I've ever asked you for anything."

There was another long pause while Porcupine thought about that.

"Yes. It is." He put his paw back in the water. Squirrel waited—and waited—and waited.

"On the high hill by the lake at sundown," said Porcupine at last. "You do the calling."

He leaned slowly farther out along the branch, his eye fixed on lunch.

With a thanks and a leap that cleared both Porcupine and his branch, Squirrel was away into the woods to spread the word.

She found the beaver first. He was a little way along the creek, repairing his lodge.

"Meeting tonight," called Squirrel, not taking the time to stop. "Meeting at sundown on the high hill. Porcupine says, 'Everyone come'."

"We have too many meetings. Too many. What's this one for?"

"Porcupine said, 'meeting.' Will you come?"

"Yes, yes, I'll come." Beaver's voice rumbled and grumbled up the creek after the squirrel. "Many too many meetings."

Groundhog said he'd be there if he could arrange to leave his burrow for five minutes, and the muskrat said he'd go and take the otter with him.

Fox was just waking from a nap, but he said,

"All right, I'll come." The fox never liked to miss anything.

On through the woods ran Squirrel, calling as she went, "Meeting tonight. Meeting tonight!" She steered clear of the snake, called to the weasel from a good safe distance, and sent the badger to find the skunk who was hunting grasshoppers at the edge of the meadow.

Squirrel scurried into the underbrush where the rabbits were, and deep down mole holes, and up by the waterfall where the raccoon was catching fish. She went high into the tamarack trees that stood on the ridge overlooking the pond, and over on the furthest edge of the forest where the moose lived. She went everywhere, and the only animal she did not find was the bear.

The bear was often sulky and bad tempered and Squirrel was not anxious to find him. But all the same she felt uneasy.

Just as the sun was setting over the lake, Squirrel and Porcupine met at the top of the hill. They looked down at the other animals climbing the path.

"I don't see the bear," said Porcupine. Squirrel didn't say anything.

The animals talked a lot as they came. They laughed, they grumbled, they shoved, and at last they all sat down in a circle.

They became silent as Porcupine stood up and made his way to the middle of the great circle. And then, before Porcupine could say a word, there was a loud thrashing in the pine trees below the hill. Bear appeared on the path. The other animals watched nervously as he climbed slowly up the path and took his place in the great circle.

Porcupine looked around at the animals. He looked at Bear. "This is Squirrel's meeting," he said. "She asked me to call it." He went back to his place and sat down.

Squirrel went and stood alone in the great circle. She knew how the animals hated the people. She knew how she'd tricked them by saying it was Porcupine's meeting. She knew how terrible Bear could be in his temper.

Then she remembered how sick the boy and all his people were.

In a small, clear voice she said, "The people are sick. We have to help them."

Above the angry cries of all the animals, Bear's growl was loudest. "What do you mean, help the people?"

For a second Squirrel didn't answer. She was too frightened to talk. Then she said, slowly, but still clearly, "In the spring when I was starving, a boy saved my life. He brought acorns and corn kernels. He is sick now. He needs our help."

Bear got up and moved toward Squirrel. The others began to move with him. The circle grew smaller.

"How dare you?" demanded the bear. "How dare you ask our help for those hunters?"

With great courage Squirrel spoke up once more. "The boy is my friend. He might die. I . . ."

Before she could finish, Bear lunged at her. The other animals were right behind, but it was Bear who grabbed Squirrel and squeezed her tightly in his forepaws.

Terrified, Squirrel bit the bear's paw. Bear roared in rage and surprise—and loosed his grip.

Squirrel leaped free, but as she escaped, Bear's claws dug deep into her back.

She ran. Faster than she had run to take the news of the meeting through the woods, faster than she'd run to find the porcupine, faster even than she'd run to fetch berries for the sick boy, she ran away from Bear and the council of the animals.

Bear came after her, but he was awkward and he stumbled. Squirrel ran under a bush. In pain and terror she hid there and waited until all the animals had stopped looking for her.

The only place she could think to be safe was the boy's wigwam. So there she went, and there she stayed for a night and a long day.

When evening came again, a small, sad, frightened squirrel crawled out of the wigwam where her silent friends were sick. She thought they would die. She thought she would die too. Bear's claws had been so sharp and had left such deep wounds along her back.

As she sat in despair in the quiet of the moonlit clearing, she heard the voice of Manitou. "You

have been a true friend, Squirrel. Speak to the
people tonight. They will understand. This is how
they can heal themselves. The pine tree, the
spruce and the balsam will give their gum. The
slippery elm will give its bark. The boy's mother
must boil these things together. When the
medicine is cool the people must all drink. Soon
they will be well."

The voice stopped. Squirrel, as quickly as she could, went back into the wigwam, wakened the mother, and told her what Manitou had said. The mother understood. With great effort she got up, and at once set about making the medicine.

When it was ready, everyone in the village had some, and in a week all the people were well.

Squirrel did not die from her wounds. They healed slowly, leaving five dark stripes along her back which she and the boy and the boy's family did not mind at all. The stripes were marks of pride.

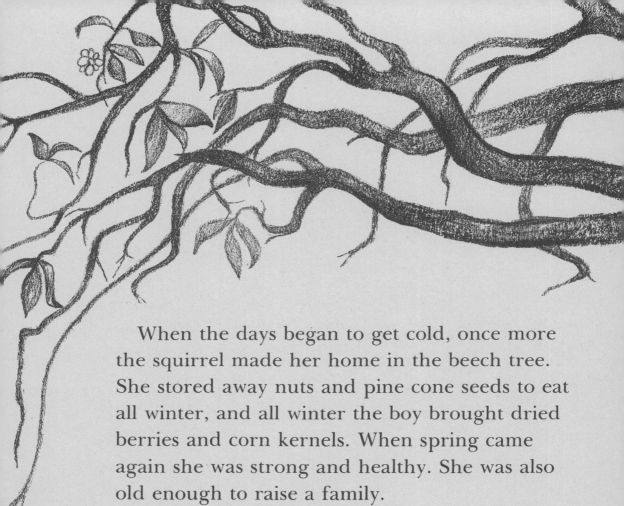

When the days began to get cold, once more the squirrel made her home in the beech tree. She stored away nuts and pine cone seeds to eat all winter, and all winter the boy brought dried berries and corn kernels. When spring came again she was strong and healthy. She was also old enough to raise a family.

The boy knew the squirrel was grown and too busy to play. He knew there would be baby squirrels, and he waited eagerly for his friend to bring them into the clearing.

Then one bright morning in spring, when leaves were on the trees and the woods were full

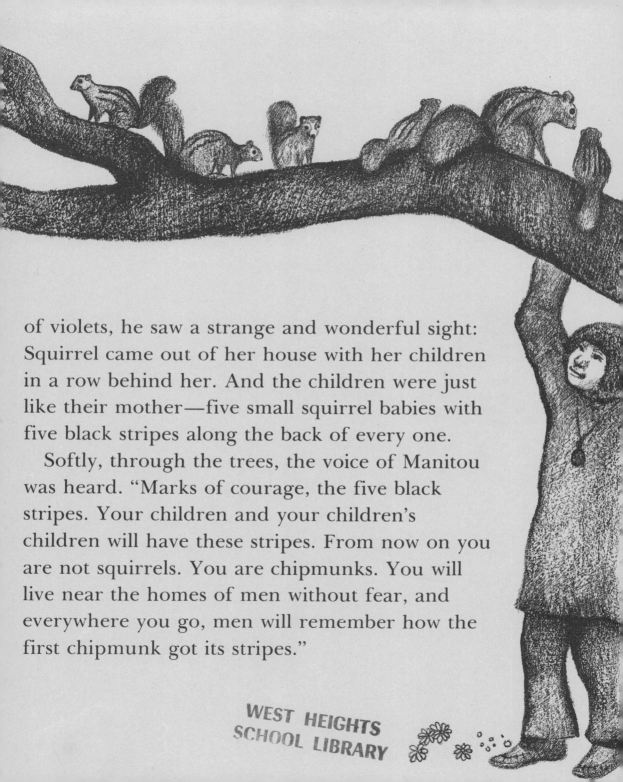

of violets, he saw a strange and wonderful sight: Squirrel came out of her house with her children in a row behind her. And the children were just like their mother—five small squirrel babies with five black stripes along the back of every one.

Softly, through the trees, the voice of Manitou was heard. "Marks of courage, the five black stripes. Your children and your children's children will have these stripes. From now on you are not squirrels. You are chipmunks. You will live near the homes of men without fear, and everywhere you go, men will remember how the first chipmunk got its stripes."

μ